"Plum-pudding dog!" the people cry,
When Prue walks out with Patch.
Prue doesn't care — she'll always wear
Her spotted dress, to match!

Now Cheeky Charlie is the name
Of Polly's Pekinese
His favourite treat is egg too yung
Because he is Chinese!

Patricia has a poodle pup,
His name is Popinjay.
Pat does *her* hair in poodle curls,
When they go out to play.

Now turn to the end of the book.

£3.15

**Printed and Published by D. C. Thomson & Co., Ltd.,
Dundee and London**

Dear Girls,
Here is another super **Twinkle Book** specially for you.
Hungry Hector, The star who lost her sparkle, Sammy's skating lesson and **The Christmas star** are just some of the great stories you will find inside.
I'm sure you'll also enjoy reading about your favourite **"Twinkle"** friends— **Nurse Nancy, Sam, My Baby Brother** and **Elfie.**
There are lots of interesting puzzles to do, too— and an exciting game to play !
Love from
Twinkle

Nurse Nancy

1 — It was almost Christmas, and Nurse Nancy and Grandad were hard at work in the hospital trying to make sure all the toys would be home for Christmas Day.

2 — However, some toys wouldn't be well enough to go home, and their owners *were* sad. To cheer up the ward, Nancy decided to put up some decorations.

3 — On Christmas Eve, the boys and girls came to the hospital to say "goodbye" to their toys. As tomorrow was Christmas Day, they would be too busy to visit them.

4 — Next day, Nancy had a lovely time, with lots of super presents. "I'll go in to the hospital later to check on the patients, Grandad," said Nancy.

5 — At the hospital, the patients looked sad. Then Nancy had an idea. "I know," she cried. "We'll have another Christmas tomorrow!"

6 — When Nancy returned home, Mummy was busy clearing the dinner table. "Can I have the leftovers, Mummy?" Nancy asked. "I'm having a Christmas party!" Mummy *was* puzzled!

7 — That evening, Nancy was *very* busy, wrapping up small Christmas presents for the toys, and telling all her friends about the special party the following day.

8 — Next day, Nancy set off early to the hospital with food and presents. All her friends brought things, too — everyone was looking forward to the party.

9 — All Nancy's chums had great fun at the party — and so did the patients. They played games, opened their presents and had a lovely Christmas meal.

10 — "It's a super idea having *two* Christmases," said Tom, whose teddy was in with a sore paw. "I think we should do the same again next year!" Everyone agreed.

Hungry Hector

ONE Christmas Eve, Hector the always-hungry reindeer was feeling especially hungry. He woke up very early, and ate every crumb of his breakfast. Then he sighed, "Is it nearly dinner time?"

"No, it isn't!" said Donald Dwarf, Father Christmas's reindeer keeper. "There's work to be done first!"

At dinner time, Hector ate all his food in a flash.

"That was nice!" he grinned. "Is it long till tea time?"

"Yes, it is!" smiled Caroline, Father Christmas's cheery cook.

"Oh dear!" groaned Hector. Then he asked, "Would you like any help?"

"No, thank you!" replied Caroline, firmly. She remembered the mess Hector had made the last time he had visited her kitchen!

At tea time, Hector ate all his own tea, then looked around in search of more.

"Well, Hector!" laughed Father Christmas sitting down to a huge plate of plum pudding. "Feeling peckish, are you?"

"I'm afraid so, Father Christmas. I think I must be growing," sighed Hector.

"I hope not!" chuckled Father Christmas. "There's enough of you to get into trouble as it is!"

Soon it was time for Father Christmas and the reindeer to get ready for their journey round the world, taking presents for all the children. Father Christmas loaded the sleigh, harnessed the reindeer to it, and took off into the sky. It was a beautiful starry night, and everything went very smoothly.

When they eventually returned home, Hector tucked eagerly into a special feed of steaming hot oat mash which Donald Dwarf had prepared for all the reindeer — but he *still* wasn't full.

"Perhaps I'll find something to eat in the garden," he muttered to himself, and quietly slipped outside. Everywhere was very dark. Hector bent his head to the ground and chewed at a tiny tree.

Suddenly, there was a frightened squeaking. "Our tree! You've eaten our Christmas tree!"

Little mice came scampering from all around.

"Oh, Hector, how could you?" sobbed a mouse called Mary.

"I'm dreadfully sorry!" said Hector. He slumped to the ground in despair. "Just when I thought I'd kept out of trouble!"

"I know!" cried a large mouse called Monty. "We could decorate Hector's *antlers*! They'd make two beautiful Christmas trees!"

So, Hector lay very still, while all the little mice scampered up and down his antlers, hanging them with tiny presents and glittering decorations.

Father Christmas laughed and laughed when he came to find Hector and give him his Christmas present.

"Happy Christmas!" he chuckled as he placed a large cake with a red H on the ground beside Hector.

Hector grinned happily at Father Christmas and started to munch his cake. "Thank you, Father Christmas!" he beamed. "How *did* you guess what to give me?"

Christmas puzzles

You can colour this picture, using your paints or crayons.

Can you spot six differences between these two Christmas trees?

Lead Katy through the maze, to reach her stocking.

Two of these parcels are exactly the same. Can you spot which ones?

Patch

1 — Paula Perkins has a cute kitten called Patch. He liked to help Paula when she fed the birds. One morning, there was no food left. "The birds are getting greedy," sighed Mummy.

There are lots of pictures of Patch hidden in the tree. How many can you find?

2 — Paula and Mummy went into the kitchen to fetch more bird food and nuts. Suddenly Patch began miaowing excitedly.

3 — Patch scampered up a tree. Paula *was* puzzled — but *she* couldn't see what Patch had spotted. It was a *squirrel* who had eaten all the birds' food — and stolen the nuts, too!

5 — Daddy knew what to do. He put the nuts in containers which he hung from the branches. "The squirrel won't be able to eat the nuts from these," he explained, "but the birds will."

4 — Patch and the squirrel playfully chased each other along the branches of the tree. How Paula and Mummy laughed. "So *that's* where all the bird food went," said Mummy.

6 — Sure enough, the birds now had plenty to eat, while Paula made sure there was food for the squirrel, too. Best of all, Patch had fun playing with his new friend!

The star who lost her sparkle

SYLVIA STAR *was* sad!

"Oh, dear!" cried Sylvia. "I've lost my sparkle and I don't know where it could be."

"I think you should travel around the world," suggested the man in the moon. "I'm sure you'll find some sparkle along the way."

And with that, the little star began her journey. The following evening, Sylvia came to a hot dusty land where the sun was just about to set.

"Perhaps the rays of the sun will spark off a few lights on me," she thought, waving to catch the sun's attention.

But the sun thought Sylvia was just waving to say, "hello!" so he politely waved back before disappearing behind the hills.

The next place Sylvia came to was a land of high mountains with snow on top and wooden chalets below. Sylvia stopped to admire the mountains.

"Perhaps I could catch a handful of that glistening snow," Sylvia thought, hopefully. "That might make me look sparkly."

Sylvia stretched down and tried to dip one of her points in the snow, but it was no use. Sylvia was too high up in the sky and although the mountain top looked so near, it was really many miles below her.

Sylvia found herself looking down at a street carnival in the dusk. It was getting dark, but the streets were still bright, because beautiful fairy lights were lining them. The fairy lights gave Sylvia an idea.

"I could carry one of those pretty lights around with me," she thought. "Then I'd twinkle in the sky."

Then, Sylvia remembered the snowy mountains from the day before.

"Those fairy lights *look* near but I know I won't be able to reach them," she thought.

So Sylvia called to a colourful parrot in the trees below and asked *him* to fetch a fairy light for her.

"I would!" the parrot replied, "but I can't fly high enough to reach you."

Sylvia thanked the parrot anyway and drifted on through the sky. She soon found herself back where she had started.

"I see you haven't found your sparkle yet, Sylvia," said the man in the moon.

"I don't think I ever will," sighed Sylvia.

Meanwhile, unknown to Sylvia, she was being watched by two children from their bedroom window in the house below.

"I bet Daddy's ship won't be home for Christmas after all," the boy said sadly.

"Well, I'm going to wish upon a star," said the girl, looking straight up at Sylvia.

As soon as the girl had made her wish, something wonderful happened. Sylvia's sparkle came back. She looked beautiful and dazzling.

"That's all it needed, Sylvia," the man in the moon smiled. "Someone to look at you and make a wish."

And the children's wish came true as well. Their daddy *did* come home for Christmas!

Thomas the tortoise

A GARDEN path seems very long
    For a slowcoach such as me.
But still I struggle on and on
    To reach a shady tree.

The day is hot, the sun is out,
    I'm feeling like a drink.
For although my house is on my back,
    It does not have a sink!

Now I'm really very lucky,
    Because I'm someone's pet.
I'm fed with lettuce leaves and such,
    And brought in when it's wet!

I don't need to eat in winter,
    So I hibernate instead,
And sleep all through the chilly days —
    You have to leave your bed!

In winter, home is a cardboard box,
    Which is packed with straw so clean.
Then I'm put into a cupboard
    Where I fall asleep and dream.

Then when the days get warmer,
    I sniff the summer air.
And rustle all my straw about
    To remind them that I'm there!

Silly Milly

1 — Silly Milly is always in trouble. Just before Christmas, while out shopping, Milly saw a Santa's Grotto.

2 — Milly couldn't wait to visit Santa, but before the silly girl could get inside, she had tangled herself in the antlers of a reindeer.

3 — When Milly finally made it into the grotto, she tripped over a pile of presents and almost knocked Santa off his seat!

4 — Once Santa had asked Milly what she would like for Christmas, he told her to choose a present from the tree.

5 — "This one I think," said Milly as she grabbed a present. However, the gift was stuck, and Milly pulled the tree over.

6 — When Mummy returned to the Grotto, there was no sign of Milly. "I wonder where she can be?" puzzled Mummy.

7 — Mummy popped inside, and when she spotted Milly, she just had to laugh.

8 — "I'm sorry," sighed Santa, "but Milly caused *so* much trouble that I couldn't think what else to do with her!" Milly was tied up securely in Santa's sack.

Polly Penguin's puzzles

Find six ice lollies hidden
on this page, then colour it in,
using your paints or crayons.

Which streamer is attached to Rodney Reindeer's antler?

Can you spot six differences between these two pictures of Willie Whale?

Can you lead Polly through the maze to join her chums for Christmas dinner?

Rearrange the letters on the Christmas cake to find out the name of Polly's cheery chum.

Uhna and the baby seal

1 — One day, while she was out fishing, Uhna, a little Eskimo girl, found a lonely baby seal. "Can I keep him, Mummy?" she asked when she returned home.

2 — Uhna's mummy agreed that the girl could keep the seal until he was strong enough to look after himself. Uhna *was* pleased, and the pair became good friends.

3 — Every day when she went fishing, Uhna took the seal with her. However, instead of catching his own fish, the seal ate the fish that Uhna caught.

4 — Mummy wasn't pleased when Uhna came home with only a few fish in her basket. "I'm afraid he'll have to go, Uhna," she said. "He has to learn to catch his own fish."

5 — Uhna was sad, but realised her mummy was right. So, the next day, she took the seal a long way from home, and left him there.

6 — The next day, Uhna went fishing, even although she didn't feel like it without the seal. She sat down on the ice at her favourite spot, and wondered if she'd ever see her chum again.

7 — Suddenly, the part of the ice she was sitting on broke off, and started to drift away into the middle of the lake. "Help! Help!" Uhna called out.

8 — But, after a while, Uhna stopped shouting, for it seemed that there was no one to hear her. The little girl was very frightened, and didn't know what to do.

9 — Then she saw several dark shapes swimming towards her — and guess what? They were seals, led by her own special friend.

10 — Together, the seals pushed the block of ice safely back to shore. "Thank you," she said to the baby seal. "I *do* wish I could take you home, but you know why I can't."

11 — The seal dived into the water again and again, filling Uhna's basket with fish. "I'm sure Mummy won't mind if you stay with us now," smiled Uhna.

12 — And of course, when Uhna returned home, and told her parents all about the clever seal, they were glad to have him stay. "He's better at catching fish than I am now," laughed Uhna.

Christmas calendar

You will need — Card, paste, scissors, a small piece of ribbon, an old Christmas card and a calendar tag.

Using one of your old Christmas cards, you can make this lovely calendar.

Just cut out the picture from one of your cards, and stick it to a stiffer piece of card to stop it from bending.

Leave a border of about 1″ all round the picture, and you can decorate this in a pretty pattern.

When you've done that, attach the calendar tag to the bottom of the card, and paste a ribbon on to the top of the card to use as a hanger. You have now completed your pretty calendar, which makes a super present for Mum and Dad!

My Baby Brother

WEE Benny's sweet, but seldom neat,
    He's full of fun and joy.
He's grubby, friendly, naughty, cute,
    Like any little boy. He's . . .

BEN loves to watch the traffic lights,
    When into town we go.
"Red, amber, green!" he calls to me.
    "I know them now, you know!"

The lighthouse has a huge, white lamp,
    That sweeps across the bay.
The lighthouse keeper showed us it,
    One summer holiday.

Ben likes the little, flashing torch
He keeps beside his bed.
"Now I'm not frightened of the dark,"
The funny fellow said.

But Benny's favourite lights are those
That twinkle on the tree.
"Look, I can see my present there!"
The scamp shouts out to me.

Race you home

The object of this fun-filled forest game is to make your way to the different homes at the end of the track.

Before you play, either cut out or trace the four animal counters on the right. Decide which animal each player wishes to be.

Now find your correct starting positions at the beginning of the track. Roll a dice and throw a six to start. Then, on the next throw, you may set off.

All along the track, you will find obstacles for each animal. The winner is the player to reach their own home first.

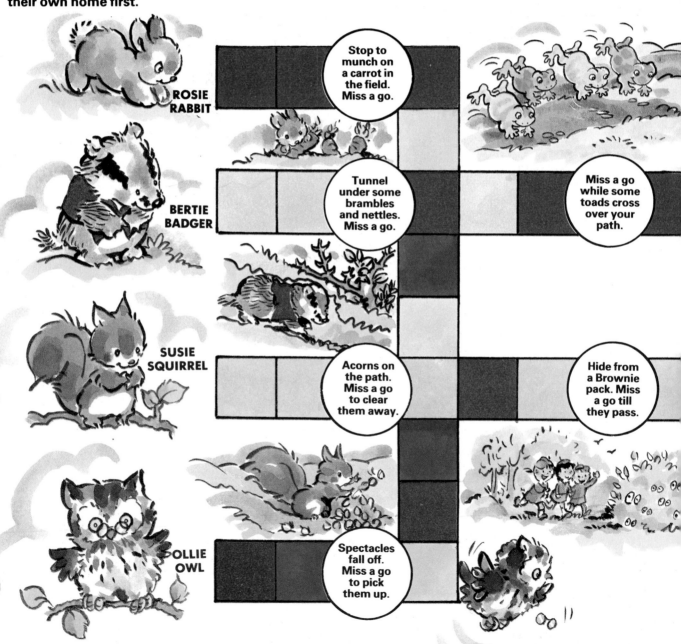

ROSIE
RABBIT

BERTIE
BADGER

SUSIE
SQUIRREL

OLLIE
OWL

Stop to
munch on
a carrot in
the field.
Miss a go.

Tunnel
under some
brambles
and nettles.
Miss a go.

Miss a go
while some
toads cross
over your
path.

Acorns on
the path.
Miss a go
to clear
them away.

Hide from
a Brownie
pack. Miss
a go till
they pass.

Spectacles
fall off.
Miss a go
to pick
them up.

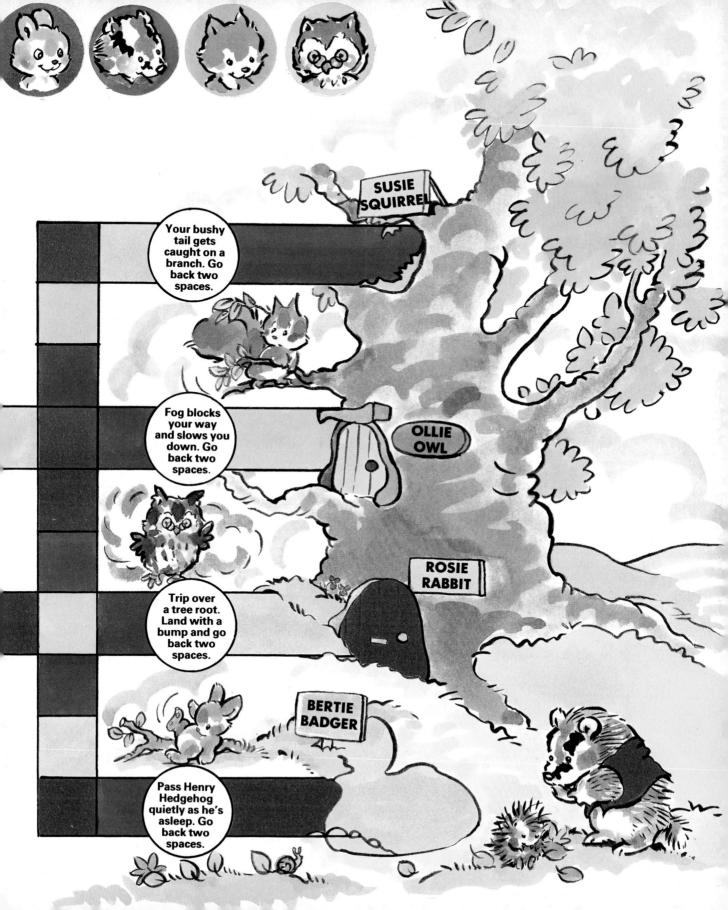

Sammy's skating lesson

1 — "Help!" cried Walter Wagtail, as he landed on the ice with a *bump!* "It's no use," said Molly Moorhen. "We'll never be able to skate." Sammy Snowman just laughed.

2 — "Maybe *I* can teach you," he said. "But how?" quacked Donna Duck, looking at his feet. "You're frozen to the ground." Sure enough, Sammy couldn't move.

3 — "Oh, dear!" said Sammy, tearfully. "I did so want to go skating." Just then, Rachael Robin flew down. Sammy told her his problem, and the little bird flew off.

4 — Rachael went to find Harry Hare and Betty Bunny, who were out playing with their sledge. The clever little bird had had an idea, and whispered it to her chums.

5 — Harry and Betty agreed to Rachael's plan, and positioned their sledge at the top of the hill. Sammy wondered what his friends were up to.

6 — The sledge went whizzing down the hill. Just as it reached the bottom, the furry friends jumped off. But the sledge kept on going, right in the direction of Sammy!

7 — Instead of knocking the snowman over, though, the sledge freed him from the ground, and carried him on to the pond. Soon Sammy was skating round the ice.

8 — Donna Duck grabbed Sammy's scarf, and all the chums followed on. "I've helped you to skate, after all," laughed Sammy, as they sped round the pond like experts.

c

Elfie

1 — Elfie lives in Mary's doll's house. Only Mary's dog, Poochie, knows about the little elf. Mary believes that the strange things Elfie makes happen are caused by magic!

2 — One day, Mary's aunt brought her a musical box. Whenever the lid was opened, music played and a little ballerina danced. "Thank you!" cried Mary. "It's *beautiful*!"

3 — Mary showed the musical box to Poochie. It wasn't just the dog who was interested. Elfie was watching, too. "I'd like to play with that," he thought.

4 — Elfie didn't have to wait long. Mary was going to visit her friend, Susan, for tea, and Poochie watched her go down the garden path. "Now's your chance, Elfie," he wuffed.

5 — When Elfie opened the box, however, he was *most* upset to discover that the ballerina wouldn't dance. "She's got stuck when Mary closed the box," he thought.

6 — Elfie knew just what to do, though. He went to the playroom and returned with his little box of tools. "I'll have it fixed by the time Mary returns," he promised Poochie.

7 — Before long, Elfie had bits and pieces of the musical box spread across the floor. He was still putting it all back together again when Poochie barked a warning.

8 — "Mary's coming back and bringing Susan with her," wuffed the dog. "Oh no — Mary will want to show Susan the musical box," gasped Elfie. "And it's not ready yet!"

9 — "There's only one thing for it, then," cried Elfie. He quickly hid his toolbox and the ballerina before *he* clambered into the musical box himself.

10 — "Now *you* must help, Poochie," Elfie shouted. "Give Mary such a welcome that Susan will have to look at the musical box on her own." Poochie *was* puzzled.

11 — However, when the girls came in, Poochie bounded over to Mary. "Gosh, you *are* pleased to see me," she laughed. Susan rushed over to the musical box alone.

12 — "It's *most* unusual," she cried. And it was — for, in place of the dancing ballerina was *Elfie*! "I'll replace the ballerina later and Mary will never know," he chuckled.

The little red balloon

IT was market day in Shilling Town and in a cottage at the edge of the town, the balloon-man was blowing up his balloons.

The balloon-man smiled when he'd finished. They were the biggest, brightest, bounciest balloons ever seen. All except one. A little red balloon called Bobby.

The balloon-man frowned when he looked at Bobby. He'd puffed and puffed but Bobby wouldn't grow any bigger.

"I can't take *you* to market," said the balloon-man. "You're *much* too small."

But Bobby looked so sad that in the end the balloon-man said, "All right — but no one will buy you."

As he walked along the lane, the big balloons bobbed and bounced and tugged at his hand, trying to break free.

In the middle of the bunch, hidden and squashed, was Bobby. But, at least, he was going to market. Surely *someone* would buy him.

On the stall next to him, a little man in a round, black hat was selling watches and clocks. They were all ticking noisily.

Curious, Bobby peeped out to see what all the noise was about. A large, cheeky clock saw him. It grinned and winked at the little red balloon and Bobby smiled back.

"Come on, boys and girls," called the balloon-man. "Buy a lovely balloon. Biggest balloons you'll ever see."

"All except me," said Bobby sadly as, one by one, the children came and took away the lovely, big balloons.

"Well," said the balloon-man at last, looking at Bobby, "it's time to go home."

But Bobby didn't want to go home. He wanted to find a little boy or girl. He looked up at the blue sky and the sailing clouds and gave a tug. It was such a little tug that the balloon-man didn't notice.

But one of the clocks on the next stall *had* noticed. Suddenly it opened its mouth and out popped a bird.

"Cuckoo! Cuckoo! Cuckoo!" called the little bird.

It made the balloon-man jump and he let go of Bobby's string. A gust of wind lifted the little balloon high into the sky.

"Tick-tock, tick-tock, goodbye," said the little clock. "And good luck."

Bobby floated high above the market-place. He saw the little man in the round, black hat putting his watches and clocks back in their boxes. He saw the big, bright balloons going home with their boys and girls.

Then the breeze took him away over rooftops and chimneys, school-yards and playing-fields.

Before long, Shilling Town was left far behind. Now the little red balloon was floating over meadows and trees and gurgling streams.

"This is fun," he cried as he chased a butterfly over the hill and into a wood.

Suddenly, he heard a sad, frightened noise. Bobby flew deeper into the wood.

He bobbed in and out of the trees, till he saw a tiny kitten, caught in a maze of creepers.

Then, he heard a little girl calling, "Oliver! Oliver! Where are you?"

Straight away, the clever little balloon flew out of the wood, and floated towards the girl.

Her name was Lucy and as she tried to catch him, he tugged out of reach.

Nearer and nearer to the wood she came, following the little balloon.

Bobby floated through the trees and showed her where the kitten was caught.

Carefully, Lucy pulled back the creepers. The kitten leapt into her arms and purred and purred and purred.

"Come on, Oliver, supper's ready," said Lucy. "Are you coming, too?" she asked the little red balloon.

This time, when she held out her hand, Bobby didn't tug away.

Floating through the sky was wonderful, but nothing was better than finding a friend — unless it was finding two.

Polly's Christmas party

1 — Polly Penguin lives in Snowland with her chums, Rodney Reindeer, Suki Seal and Peter Polar Bear. One day, very near Christmas, Polly handed out invitations.

2 — "I want you to come to my party," she said to Suki, Rodney and Peter. "We'll have a super time." The chums could hardly wait, Polly's parties were always great fun.

3 — On the day of the party, Polly began to blow up balloons and hang streamers. She baked lots of tasty cakes and bought bottles of fizzy pop.

4 — Suki was the first to arrive. "Brrr!" she said as she handed Polly her coat, hat and scarf. "It's cold today." Polly was about to reply when the doorbell rang again.

5 — Very soon, poor Polly was hidden beneath all the coats and scarves. "Oh, dear," she puffed as she tried to move about. "I don't have anywhere to put them."

6 — "Perhaps I can help," said Rodney Reindeer politely. "Polly was puzzled until Rodney explained his plan. Soon the little penguin was free to move about the house.

7 — Helpful Rodney had told Polly to pile the clothes on his antlers. Soon the scarves and hats were safely out of the way and everyone could enjoy the party.

8 — "This is a super party," said the chums. "Yes," said Polly, "and it's thanks to Rodney we can all enjoy it without falling over our outdoor clothes. Merry Christmas everyone!"

Emily's wish

EMILY ELEPHANT watched her mummy as she rehearsed in the circus ring. The little elephant looked very proud as her mum carried the ballerina on her back.

"You look very beautiful, Mummy," she said proudly.

"I wish *I* could perform in the Big Top," said Emily. "I would love to entertain the children," she sighed.

"Never mind," whispered her mummy. "You'll soon be big enough to come into the ring with me."

Emily smiled. "Oh, I hope so!" she cried.

The next day, Mr Watts, the ringmaster, came to fetch Emily.

"Come on, Emily!" he cried, "I want you to do some tricks."

"Go on," said her mummy, gently. "Now's your big chance."

The little elephant was taken to a corner of the ring to practise. She tried to balance a chair on her trunk, but it landed on the floor with a *crash!*

2 — "Oh, dear!" sighed Emily, as she was taken back to her trailer in disgrace. "I'll *never* be able to entertain in the Big Top. The trainer says I'm hopeless," she sobbed. "No one will ever want to see a stupid elephant like me. Why can't I be clever and beautiful, like my mummy?"

Emily was very upset, and cried herself to sleep.

3 — A few days later, Emily and her mummy were led into a big truck. The big elephant looked very sad, and Emily hated to see her mummy so upset.

"What's the matter?" asked the little elephant.

"They're closing down the circus," replied her mummy. "They can't afford to keep it open any longer."

"Does that mean you won't be performing any more?" asked Emily.

"I'm afraid so."

"But what's going to happen to us?" said the little elephant, in a worried voice.

"I don't know," said her mummy. "We'll just have to wait and see."

4 — The elephants travelled many miles inside the noisy truck, until finally it stopped. When they stepped outside, Emily's mummy was delighted.

"It's a zoo!" she cried, excitedly.

The little elephant was taken to a grassy parkland, where lots of children were waiting to meet her. Two of the children were lifted on to Emily's back, all ready for an *elephant* ride!

"I'm not useless at all," cried Emily, happily. "And I'm entertaining children at last!"

Paper plate

You can make lots of super things with paper plates — we're going to show you just a few of them. You will need plates, glue, crepe paper, pens and paints, wool, streamers, cotton wool, rice, scissors, card, a cotton reel and felt.

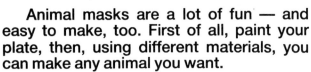

Animal masks are a lot of fun — and easy to make, too. First of all, paint your plate, then, using different materials, you can make any animal you want.

To make the lion, cut up strips of crepe paper, and paste them behind the plate. Use card for ears, and use pens or paints for the face.

An owl can be made using card for its ears and beak. Eyes can be painted on or made from card.

A sheep is fun to do — stick down cotton wool for its fleece, and felt for floppy ears. Using a black felt pen, draw in eyes, a nose and mouth.

If you'd like to make the cat, cut up strands of wool for whiskers, and glue them down. Ears can be made from card or felt. Other features can be painted on.

Put two holes either side of the mask, thread a piece of elastic through and knot the end. Remember to cut out holes for the eyes.

Now your mask is ready to wear.

To make a skimmer, decorate two paper plates any way you like, then glue the rims together.

To make this piggy bank, paint two plates a pale pink, then draw a face on one of them. Next, make a hole for a nose, the size of a cotton reel, and a slit for money. Glue the rims of the plates together, pasting felt or card for ears between them. Insert the cotton reel into position. And now you have a super piggy bank. To get your money out, simply remove the cotton reel.

If you'd like to make this tambourine, brightly decorate two paper plates. Next, cut up strips of streamers, crepe paper or ribbon. Paste these between the plates, which should also contain a handful of rice. Finally, glue the rims of the plate together.

The Christmas star

1 — The box of Christmas decorations were getting excited. "Christmas is almost here," the little star said excitedly. "My toes are tingling."

2 — The pixies were too excited to keep still, and got in a terrible muddle. One of them caught his foot in the loop on the star's back, and pulled it clean off!

3 — The next day, little Joy opened the box. "Mummy," called Joy, "the star is broken!" "Never mind," said Mummy, "I've bought some new decorations."

4 — Joy put the little star back in the old box and put the new angel on top of the tree. The other toys looked at each other sadly. "Poor star," they thought.

5 — Next day, Joy was sad. She was the fairy in the Christmas play, but her wand had broken. "Don't worry," said Mummy, "we'll make a new one."

6 — Together, Daddy and Joy made a lovely new wand, and right on top, in pride of place, sparkled the little star. He *was* pleased at having a special Christmas job to do.

7 — The school play was the next day. The little star was very excited. And as Joy waved her wand, the star sent twinkles of starlight through the air.

8 — That night, Joy hung her wand on the tree. "But where have you been?" asked his chums. "To Fairyland!" said the star. "Happy Christmas, everyone."

Sam

SHONA MACGREGOR and her sheepdog, Sam, live in the Scottish Highlands.

The little girl and her friends had lots of fun playing in the countryside around their homes — especially during winter when the snow lay deep on the ground.

One day, during the Christmas holidays, Shona was out sledging with Sam and her friend Moira Harris. Sam enjoyed the fun as much as the girls!

"Do you remember that den we built in the summer?" Moira asked her chum. "Let's go and see if we can find it."

The girls hurried off to the spot where they had built their den, but on the way there, they stopped in surprise. A young fox was blocking their path.

2 — "Isn't it strange — he's not running away from us!" cried Shona.

"I don't think he's well, Shona," her friend remarked. "He looks thin and tired."

Shona decided that they should call Moira's father, the local vet.

3 — "He's healthy enough," Mr Harris told the girls after he had examined the fox. "But he's very hungry."

The fox gobbled up the meat that Mr Harris fed to him.

"Isn't he a little young to be without his parents?" Shona asked.

Mr Harris explained to the girls that during the winter, young dog foxes were chased away by their parents, to start to fend for themselves.

"I'm afraid this one just isn't ready," he told them. "I'll look after him here until he's well again."

4 — After a few days, the fox was much better, and Mr Harris set it free. However, instead of running off, the fox stayed where he was — he didn't want to leave.

"He knows he'll be looked after if he stays here," remarked Mr Harris. "But he has to learn to look after himself."

Mr Harris didn't know *what* to do.
Just then, Sam set off into the countryside.

"Whatever is he up to?" Shona wondered. "We'd better follow him."

5 — The girls followed Sam into the woods, and soon found out what he had in mind.

"Look!" cried Shona. "Sam's found the den we made to play in in the summer. I think Sam is trying to give the fox an idea."

And sure enough, the fox, who had followed Sam to the den, soon made it his home.

The girls gave the fox some food to help him settle into his new den.

Soon, however, the fox started to find his own food, and Shona and Moira knew he would be all right.

"Well done, Sam," Shona told her dog. "I'm sure our fox will survive the winter snow."

Buzzy

It was the hive Christmas party, and Buzzy was helping with the decorations.

Could you go and find some mistletoe?

Buzzy searched high and low . . . .

. . . but she couldn't find mistletoe anywhere!

I'll just have to enjoy the party without it.

Suddenly

BIG KISS

Tee hee! I couldn't find the mistletoe, but it found me!

Jack Frost's puzzles

You can colour this picture, using your paints or crayons.

Can you spot six differences between these two pictures?

Lead Dinah Duck through the maze to her chum, Desmond.

Which two snowflakes are exactly alike?

14. 12. 10.
13. 9. 8.
11.
15. 7. 6.
16.
17. 5.
19. 4.
18. 3.
20. 1.
2.

Join the dots to complete this star.

Which length of frost is about to freeze the puddle?

A

B

C

Ans:- A.

Diana's ducklings

1 — Diana lived in the country with her mummy and daddy. At the bottom of their garden was a shallow brook. Diana would often paddle in it.

2 — One day, Diana decided to build a dam in the brook. She collected some twigs and stones and piled them up in the water. The water birds *were* puzzled by Diana's game.

3 — Later, Diana spotted a nest of baby ducks. "I'd love to play with them," sighed Diana, "but I don't imagine their mother would let me."

4 — One day, though, it began to rain very hard. Diana's dam began to cause problems in the brook. The water ran fast and flooded over the banks.

5 — When the rain stopped, Daddy, Mummy and Diana ventured outside. Diana rushed to the brook, in time to see the ducklings being carried away.

6 — "Oh, no!" shouted Diana. "Save them, Daddy." But the nest had passed before he could reach it. The nest sped on, until luckily it came to rest on Diana's dam.

7 — "Your dam may have caused a flood," chuckled daddy, "but it certainly saved those baby ducks. Mrs Duck *will* be pleased."

8 — Daddy was right. Everyday when Diana visited the brook, Mrs Duck allowed her babies to go and play with the little girl. She knew they would be safe with Diana, their new playmate.

Becky, Ben and Boots

1 — Becky and Ben Carter have a cute Shetland pony called Boots. One day, they all went to the fair together. Becky and Ben *did* have fun — but Boots didn't.

2 — The little pony was sad because he couldn't join in. After Becky and Ben had been on the roundabout, they bounced on the inflatable castle. Boots could only watch.

3 — Later, they took Boots with them into the Hall of Magic Mirrors. Becky and Ben *did* laugh at the funny shapes the mirrors made — but Boots *still* wasn't happy.

4 — The little pony stared at one mirror in particular. It seemed to show a very thin pony that was just a sack of bones. Boots didn't realise it was really only him!

5 — "Laughing makes me hungry — let's have a hamburger," chuckled Becky. "Good idea!" agreed Ben. But as they munched, they didn't notice what Boots was up to.

6 — The pony grabbed a bag of buns in his mouth and trotted away from the stall. The owner *wasn't* pleased! "Come back, you thieving nag," he shouted angrily.

7 — But Boots didn't run far. He trotted back to the Hall of Magic Mirrors and gave the bag of buns to the startled doorman. "*Now* I understand," laughed Becky.

8 — Boots had taken the bag of buns for the very thin pony he'd seen in the mirror! Even the stall owner laughed — and he fed Boots a bun for his good intentions.

Wanda's magic spectacles

W ANDA WITCH was in a panic. She'd been all ready to start making the hair-growing potion for Mr Perrywinkle, when she'd discovered she'd lost her spectacles.

"What am I going to do?" she cried. "I can't read the spell book without them."

She looked in the sooty cauldron, under the bed, in the teapot, under the settee, in the biscuit barrel, and everywhere else she could think of. Books flew here, cushions flew there.

Wanda was in a right old tizzy and she didn't care *who* knew it.

Her little black cat, Nettle, climbed on top of the broomstick cupboard, and sucked the tip of his tail. He always did that when he was worried.

"Bats wings and toads tongues," Wanda grumbled. "They must be *somewhere*."

Then she let out a loud screech which made poor Nettle's hair stand on end.

"Of course, of course, that's it!" Wanda yelled. "They must have fallen out of my pocket when I collided with Barney Owl."

She picked a broomstick up off the floor and poked Nettle off the top of the cupboard.

"Stop hiding, Nettle, and tell me where we were when we collided with Barney Owl," she commmanded.

Nettle picked himself up out of the coal scuttle where he'd landed, and replied wearily, "We were flying over the garden of Cherry Tree Cottage, mistress."

"Ah!" cried Wanda Witch. "Then tonight we'll go back to Cherry Tree Cottage and find my spectacles."

But the spectacles had already been found.

"How very strange," Abigail Summers was saying at that very moment in the garden of Cherry Tree Cottage. "I'm sure I hid my glasses at the bottom of my toy box."

Abigail hated wearing her glasses at school. One boy, Mark Weston, delighted in deliberately bumping into her and saying, "Watch where you're going, Four Eyes!"

Abigail had no time to do anything but push the specs case into her bag and hurry off to school.

She managed to get into the classroom without seeing the horrible Mark Weston.

"Get your number books out, children," Miss Sweet, her teacher, said. "And, Abigail — put your glasses on."

Abigail took the spectacle case out of her bag. She opened it, and then she gasped. The glasses *looked* exactly like her own, but in the lid of the case was a name . . . and it wasn't hers.

"Wanda Witch," Abigail read, tingling with excitement. "If these really belong to a witch, perhaps they're *magic*."

She put the glasses on and opened her number book.

"I wish all my sums were finished," she said to herself. In a second, the blank page was filled with sums. Abigail was delighted.

Abigail had a *lovely* day. Miss Sweet even asked her to feed Fluff, the school pet rabbit.

Abigail hurried into the field where Fluff lived in a large, comfortable cage. She was just giving him a cuddle, when a voice startled her.

"Well, if it isn't Four Eyes."

Abigail swung round to face Mark Weston and, as she did so, Fluff leapt out of her arms, and ran behind some bushes.

"Now see what you've done," Mark laughed nastily. "Lost the bunny?"

For a moment, Abigail's tummy turned a somersault, but then she remembered the magic spectacles.

"I haven't lost Fluff at all," she retorted. "Now leave me alone — or else I'll set Fluff on you! My glasses are magic."

"Magic!" snorted Mark. "Go on, then. Let's see you do some magic."

Abigail smiled. "I wish Fluff was as big and as fierce as a lion," she thought.

Suddenly, there was a rustling behind the bushes.

"Come here, Fluff," Abigail called. An enormous, fierce-looking Fluff came padding out, growling softly.

Mark stopped giggling.

"HELP!" he yelled, backing away. "Keep him off."

Fluff took a step nearer Mark and growled again. Mark didn't wait any longer. He turned and ran. Abigail felt very happy. She knew Mark wouldn't dare to bother her any more, so long as she wore her glasses.

That night, Wanda Witch and Nettle went back to Cherry Tree Cottage to get the spectacles. When Abigail woke up the next morning, she found they had gone from the bedside table where she'd put them.

She went over to her toy box and fished out her own glasses.

"Mark will never know the difference," she chuckled.

Meanwhile, Wanda Witch was taking hers off. She put a bottle of black, gooey stuff by her broomstick.

"That should do the trick, Nettle," she said. "Mr Perrywinkle will now get a fine crop of hair. We'll deliver it tonight."

But Nettle was already fast asleep.

Diana has a dachshund,
    He's very long and thin.
I always call him sausage dog,
    Which makes Diana grin!

Beth has a labrador, called Luke,
    They go for walks each day.
Beth has to hang on tight, because
    It's Luke who leads the way!

Nurse Nancy is my special friend,
    She has a spaniel pup.
Sometimes, she takes him round the wards,
    To cheer the patients up.